DEATH WITCH NEW WITCH

THE CRAFT OF VENGEANCE

LILI BLACK

LITERARY & SERVICES

www.llliteraryservices.com

Copy Editing by L&L Literary Services, LLC

Printed in the United States of America.

ISBN: 978-1-953437-66-2

First Printing, 2021

ALSO BY LILI BLACK

SERIES BY LILI BLACK

Accidentally Dead

Children of the Shifting Gods

Manberry Witches

Museum of Magic, Mayhem, and Wonder

Spearwood Academy

For More Books by These Authors, Check Out

www.authorliliblack.com

1

Donovan's hands shake as he stands and cradles the jar with his mother's heart in his arms. When he lifts his head, heat crackles through the air, and I know he's ready to burn the cabin and all the horrors it holds down to the ground because that same fire burns through me.

I grab his arm to draw his attention. "We can't burn this place down, and..." My teeth sink into my lips, leaving a cooper taste in my mouth before I continue, "We can't take the hearts with us."

"What?" he roars, his face darkening as he shakes his arm free. "Taking out all of this is the first step to undermining my father."

My stomach swims from nausea, but I hold firm, hoping he'll hear me out. "He can't know we're on to him. I've only been seriously studying magic for a couple of years, and before that, I was useless. Our only chance to defeat him is the element of surprise. Ripping apart this bunker with his treasures in it will tip him off."

"And he may have more bunkers out there." Donovan runs a hand through his brown hair. "This is a source of his power, though. We have to cut him off from it."

The lump in my stomach grows as Donovan sets his mom's heart back on the shelf.

"I don't know how to do that," I say in a meek voice.

My confidence in coming here wanes as what we found in this room presses in on me. How can someone be this far into the darkness? I thought I touched on black magic, but I now laugh at my efforts. I was like a child in the kiddy pool compared to the depths this man is capable of.

The contents of this room completely destroy all of the planning I've done up until now. I was a fool to think I could take on the coven that destroyed my family. A sense of defeat washes over me, making me tremble with an overwhelming desire to give up. We've already lost. Maybe Donovan has the right idea. We should just take our families' hearts, destroy this place, and call it a win.

"—ine. Evaine. Sabine!" Donovan yells as he wraps an arm around my shaking shoulders.

The contact clears my mind, and I focus on his green eyes. Those eyes used to hold all the joy and love I craved, but now, they're as empty as I feel.

"We have to get out of here." Donovan tugs me against his chest. "Do you feel that magic? I think we set off a ward or something. There's an oppressive pressure on my mind to just lie down and give up."

Now that he pointed it out, I realize the chill settling into my bones isn't all from the underground coolness of the room. Without a second thought, I summon the dark grimoire. It lands on the floor in front of me with a thud. I'm a little shocked it could make it through the wards, but this tome holds centuries of power within its pages. This room isn't old enough to block it.

We kneel together, and Donovan asks, "What kind of spell are you considering?"

A dry laugh escapes my lips. "Normally, the book finds the spell for me."

Brows raised, Donovan nods and leaves me to the book as I open the cover and hover my hands over it. The pages flip and land on a diversion spell.

"This has to be where the concept of an incubus and succubus comes from." I read the passage to him.

Donovan leans closer and rereads the passage. "So, this spell takes power from one person and gives it to another?"

"That's the way it sounds. If we can transfer some, if not all, of this energy to us, then we not only weaken your father but boost our power. We'll still have to come up with a plan, but this would be a good start."

The spell sounds simple. From what I've found, there's no rhyme or reason to spells. Actions like this, which provide the wielder with tremendous power, don't have many steps, whereas some spells, which seem simple, require multiple steps. The simplicity of the spell is the part that makes it impossible, though.

"I don't think I can do this." I push the book back and drop my head.

"Why? What is it asking?" Donovan asks.

I glance up at him, brows pinched together. "We have to be given a part of the person or object, then burn it with our blood. Your dad isn't going to give us anything, and the objects in here are parts of people or covens."

Donovan holds up the jar with his mom's heart in it. "I'll do it. My mom gave me her heart when I was born. At least, that's what she used to tell me when I was little."

We both had horrible childhoods. Even though I understand why my mom pushed me the way she did and treated me differently from the others, it still hurts. I can't say she ever gave me her heart, because she shared that with everyone in the coven. Donovan's dad pushed him hard to be something he's not, but at least his mother was there, for a while, to comfort him.

"Are you sure?" Most would struggle with that level of sacrifice. Not his father, obviously, but Donovan is offering to destroy the last remaining piece of a mother who he loved and who loved him in return.

"Yes. No... Maybe?" Donovan looks up at the jar. "She wouldn't want this. She was a white witch, like your mom. She wouldn't want to be part of a spell meant to harm, but at the same time, she'd hate that her power is feeding black magic. I need to release her"—he sweeps his arm in front of the shelf full of hearts—"and all the others, from his clutches. She can't rest until I do. None of them can."

I nod in understanding. My mom bound her

sister's magic and, in turn, my magic, to stop black magic from spreading. She'd hate all of this as well.

"Do you think you can handle the power? I don't know how much is here, but it's a lot. It may overwhelm you." I almost drop to my knees, remembering the weight of the magic passing into and through me from just my coven, and there are so many more here. "My family diverted their magic to me to stop your dad from taking it. Maybe others were able to do the same with their magic."

"What if you need the magic for something?" Donovan paces, not really expecting an answer. It feels more like he's talking to himself as he tries to decide what to do.

On his third pass, he stops in front of an intricately carved, wooden box. The carvings are inlaid with mother of pearl, which makes them look alive as the light bounces across them.

He runs his fingers over the lid, tracing the different patterns.

"Do you know what that is?" I ask.

"It's my mother's jewelry box. My grandmother gave it to her when I was born." Donovan cracks open the lid and lifts out a mother of pearl ring. "I forgot about this." He twists the ring in the light. "My grandmother said the ring was meant to protect my mother's children."

Expression twisting with grief, his eyes drop. I want to wrap my arm around him, but now, isn't the time. We have so much to talk through before I'm ready to comfort him.

"It's beautiful," I say instead.

Donovan wipes his nose on his sleeve and straightens. "We need to transfer the magic to the ring. That way, either of us can tap into it. My mom would want both of us to be protected from the hate my father is spreading throughout the world."

Unsure about using something so precious, I bite my lip. I don't know if I'd have the strength to sacrifice one of my family's artifacts since. There are so few things left for me to connect to those I lost.

"I don't know," I say at last. "I'm still trying to get the hang of the magic I already hold, and dark magic is new to you as well. I'd feel horrible if we destroyed the ring because we don't know what we're doing."

"I believe in us." His resolve hardens as he closes the lid to the jewelry box.

Taking his mother's heart back off the shelf, he collects an incense burner resting on one of the shelves and walks to a small workbench in the room.

"We should be careful with that incense burner,"

I caution. “We don’t know where it came from. What happens if we trigger something when we use it?”

My mom and grandmother kept the magic items in our coven locked in our vault most of the time. For classes and rituals, they brought out only what was needed. We rarely had magic imbued items lying around. Hattie kept a few things in her room, but most of those were locked away or hidden.

From birth, I was always taught that the smallest things could set off magic, especially if strong emotions are tied to the intent behind someone’s action. For the longest time, I was afraid to touch anything in the house for fear of blowing the place up as I stomped around, angry all the time.

Reluctantly, Donovan sets his mom’s heart and ring down on the workbench. When he only holds the burner, he closes his eyes and runs his hand over it. “It’s clean. There’s no magic associated with it.”

“Really?” Surprise comes through my voice. “You can tell?”

I received lessons on this type of thing, but since my magic was suppressed, I never managed to master the skill and forgot how to even go about checking.

“I’ll show you how.” Donovan hands me the burner, then steps up behind me, his chest warming my back. He pushes my hair to the side as he reaches around me to hold my other hand. "Close your eyes and concentrate on the object."

Pulse racing at his nearness, I close my eyes, and he waves my hand over the object. I can't concentrate, though, lost as his familiar scent envelops me. Despite the danger of his dad arriving any minute to catch us, I relax against Donovan. For the first time in a long while, my heart opens up to the possibility that this will work out in the end. I may not have to sacrifice myself to destroy the monster who took everything from me. I'm not alone.

"Are you focusing?" he asks, his breath a whisper across my ear.

"Yes," *on you*, I amend in my head.

A shiver runs down my spine as I shift my mind away from Donovan and back to the object. My shoulders droop when I feel nothing from the incense burner.

"Let me help." Donovan links his fingers through mine.

Momentarily, I'm lost in the buzz of his magic flowing through my fingers. He moves my hand again, and I concentrate on the area. His magic lights up through me, but in doing so, I catch onto the pull to the burner. Subdued heat radiates from it, but it's all natural; no magic was used with this object.

My hand, still linked with his, flies to my mouth. "I feel it. It has no magic."

Excited that I performed a spell I failed as a child, I spin to look at him.

His green eyes lock with mine for a moment before he steps back. "It's a handy trick to have, not that I'd recommend walking around checking every object for magic, but if you're going to use a magical item for something, it's good to know what properties it holds."

He takes the incense burner from my hand and places it on the workbench next to the heart and ring.

"Do you think the ring will withstand the magic we're going to add to it, since it's already embedded with magic?" My gut tightens again at the thought of destroying his mom's ring.

"It will be fine since we aren't changing the underlying magic of the ring. If we were trying to make a fire object into a water object, we'd have to strip the first magic to apply the new one," he explains. "With this, we're taking its protection properties and enhancing them to strip power from our enemies to give us that power. The ring wants to help us."

Donovan places the white, silver, and light green ring into the middle of the burner, then he takes out his pocketknife. His hand shakes as it hovers over the jar. Before I can say anything, he breaks the seal, slides the knife into the liquid that preserves the heart, then carves a small piece off the backside. The knife hooks into the tough muscle, and he pulls the piece out of the jar, placing it on top of the ring inside the incense bowl.

Unsure how to help, I stand next to him and watch.

Once he's finished the setup, he wipes the blade on a rag laying on the bench. When the rag sizzles and smokes, I jump back.

"We need to destroy both of those," I say as I step back into place.

Donovan wraps the knife in the now blackened rag. "Do you have a knife we can use for the blood portion? I wouldn't want to use anything left in here."

I can't agree with that fast enough. I have no doubt his dad would figure out how to use even the faintest trace of blood given the chance.

Sliding the scissors from my pocket, I hold them out. "These will work."

He doesn't take them. "We should both give our blood."

"That won't work. It's your mom's heart with your blood." I hold the scissors back out to him.

"It will work." His eyes light up as they lock onto mine. "I gave my heart to you a while ago. We're all linked, now."

My chest tightens with emotion. Not now. I can't deal with my feelings right now, maybe never. But if we can both tap into his magic, we'll be better off in the end. "Okay."

"Okay."

I prick my finger first, the blood beading up on the end of it. Passing the scissors to him, he follows suit. Once we both have enough pooled blood, we turn our hands over and drip the blood onto the piece of heart and the ring. Just as the blood hits, we both direct fire into the bowl. It flares a bright blue.

When the flames die down, only the ring remains, the colors darkening to black, copper, and emerald green.

2

The ring was beautiful before, reflecting the light through its depths. Now, it swirls with color, but instead of the light shining through it, it seems to pull light into it, leaving shadows in its wake.

Donovan picks up the ring. From the way he turns it my way, I know he'll try to get me to take it, but I'm not ready for that. Even though the ring will give him a power advantage, I have no desire to take it from him. It would be like giving him my scissors. The ring is a link to his mother.

Placing my hand on his bicep, I stop him. "You should wear the ring. We may need some extra power to get out of here."

He's reluctant to put the ring on, but in the end,

he slides it onto his finger anyway. A small shiver runs through him, which I choose to ignore. With this step complete, we need to get moving. We spent more time down here than I planned, and it put us at risk of the guard waking up.

Picking up the incense burner, I place it in the middle of what remains of the rag and wrap it and the pocketknife into it before I grab the dark grimoire.

Donovan gently places the lid back onto the heart. We can't fix the seal, but hopefully, his dad won't look too closely at it. I'm also worried that the damage we did, not only by opening it but cutting it, may destroy it.

We can't change that now, though, and I don't want to voice my thoughts to Donovan. This trip has been hard enough for him.

Once he places the jar back onto the shelf, we check the room to make sure we didn't disturb too much, then we leave and shut the door. The trip back out of the hidden room is quick, and Donovan insists on climbing up the ladder first. We don't know what we're walking into. The guard may have already woken up and alerted Donovan's dad to the intruders.

He cracks open the hidden door slowly, and light

filters in from above. It seemed like we were down there all day, but the sun is still bright in the sky. The coast must be clear because he pushes the trapdoor open and climbs out.

The door to the outhouse is still closed, but Donovan strides over to look inside, just to be safe. Even from where I stand, I can see the forest ranger's relaxed feet laying limp against the floor. Closing the metal door, I move the front step to the cabin back in place. A click sounds, and the step sucks in flush to the cabin, the same as it had been when we arrived. To a casual observer, no one would know we'd been down there.

Satisfied, I walk over to join Donovan at the outhouse.

"How are we going to hide this? Your dad is going to know someone was here if we can't figure out how to keep him quiet." I nudge the guard with my foot, and he doesn't even twitch.

Worried, I bend to check for a pulse. He still has one, so we didn't kill him. I sigh with relief. Even though I plan on killing Gregory Crawford for what he did to my family, I don't want to go around murdering everyone who works for or with him.

Donovan runs his hands through his hair,

causing it to stand out at funny angles. "Does that grimoire have any suggestions?"

The lure of the dark grimoire pulls at me, begging me to use it. So far, I've managed to ignore some of the darker suggestions, but each time I open it, that desire to resist lessens. If we just use it a few more times, though, it shouldn't hurt anything.

Donovan takes the burned clothe with the tools we used to free up my hands.

Resting the book on my upturned palms, I picture what I want. The guard to forget we were here. The guard forgetting anyone was here. As I firm up the image in my head, the grimoire flips open to a spell.

I read the offered page and almost throw up. "The grimoire suggests a death spell. It tends to start with the darkest spells first, which I guess I should expect since it's born from the darkest of magic."

"Ask again. It's bound to have something else," he suggests.

Summoning the image again, I hook my fingers into the pages and open to a new spell. This one puts the recipient into a permanent coma and fills his dreams with his greatest nightmares. That probably would have been an interesting spell for Macey, but feels too extreme here.

Frustrated, I try again.

With my nerves almost at their end, I flip to a new page and read the spell.

"Finally," I breathe out, the weight on my chest lifting briefly. The newest spell causes temporary amnesia of the last quarter of the day.

Donovan shifts position to read the page over my shoulder. "I think this will work." He looks at his watch. "We haven't been here for six hours, so he won't remember anything that happened while we were here."

Reading over the spell, my hands shake as I realize what I have to do. Setting the book down, I pull my scissors out, but Donovan snatches them before I can go further.

"I'll do it," he volunteers, and his aura darkens.

Neither of us were on a path to be dark witches, but this is where fate led us. At this point, we'll both be nothing but a shell of what we were if we let the darkness settle too deeply.

"No. You did the last one. It's my turn. We need to share the burden of this equally, or we won't be able to handle the coming storm." I hold my hand out, and Donovan reluctantly places the handle of the scissors onto my palm.

The spell requires that I carve a memory rune

into the guard's forehead, only the rune needs to be drawn backward with the intent to forget and not to remember. Donovan sets the rag and incense burner on the ground, then helps pull the sleeping guard upright. Grasping his jaw, Donovan holds his head firmly in place. We don't want to risk messing up. I slap another sleep spell on him, too, just to be safe. The last thing we need is for the guard to wake up from the pain before I can finish.

Glancing down at the open grimoire, I review the drawing again. Messing up a rune can be just as bad —if not worse—than him waking up or killing him. I take a shaky breath to steady my nerves and place the sharp blade of the scissors against the guard's forehead. Applying pressure, I move the blade in a swirling pattern, tracing the diagram into his skin. If I'm careful, the lines will be fluid, and I won't have to lift the blade off until I'm done.

Blood drips down his face and around his nose as I work. Throughout the process, the guard remains disturbingly still, with no sign he feels a thing. Once I finish, I lift the blade away and summon earth magic to settle into the rune, then follow it with a touch of fire, which makes the rune glow slightly.

When the glow subsides, the rune sinks into the

man's skin, sucking his blood up with it. No evidence of what we did remains on his forehead.

"Should we put him back in his truck?" Donovan asks. "Or leave him here?"

"Leave him here," I say as I crouch and wipe my scissors on the rag from the basement. "He'll know something's up, anyway, when he realizes his weapon is missing and he's lost a quarter of the day. We need to hurry and get out of here. We're lucky no one else has shown up. Someone will be looking for him, soon, if they're not already."

As Donovan locks the guard back up in the outhouse, I check the site for anything we may have done that could lead back to us. There isn't anything we can do about the tire tracks, but the treads from the forest ranger's SUV overlays ours. We just have to hope that they'll blend together enough that we won't be followed. I place the rag bundle in the back of Donovan's SUV, then climb into the front seat as he slides behind the wheel.

"Where should we go now?" Donovan looks around anxiously as he performs a U-turn and drives out to the main street.

"Let's go back to the trailer. It's the safest place I know. It will also give us a chance to regroup." We drive in silence most of the way there, only breaking it for me to give him directions.

As when we pull into the campsite, the atmosphere hangs heavily around us. We found what we're looking for, but it gives me no peace. Donovan's darkening aura worries me, too.

While I work on bringing the fire back to life in the pit, I keep an eye on him as he walks into the woods. But I don't follow. He needs space right now to process. I've had years to come to terms with everything that happened, but he's had a lot thrown at him in a short amount of time.

The grief on his face when he found his mother's heart nearly broke me, and I vow we'll get her heart back, along with my coven's. They deserve proper burials.

With both my mind and body drained, I just want to curl up and sleep, but I make some dinner first, grabbing oats from the dry storage in the cave, then water and bowls from the camper.

We'll have to buy supplies soon, but the thought of venturing into town scares me. What if someone realizes what we've done? The darkness that's been consuming me is now doing the same to Donovan. Any witch close to us will be able to feel it.

Which begs the question of why Donovan didn't

know I was a witch sooner. Does he not see the darkness the way I do?

"What has you so pensive?"

I scream a little as Donovan walks into the firepit area, then I pick up a pebble and toss it at him. "Don't scare me like that!"

"Sorry. I tried to make noise as I was coming back, but you seemed pretty focused." He sits next to me on his log.

I surprise myself by considering it his now. He has a place here with me, just as Hattie did. "I was just thinking about how..."

Do I tell him what I've seen? Will that make it worse?

"About how...What?" He scoops some of the gruel into a bowl I set out for him and takes a bite, not complaining about the runny mixture.

"Sorry about dinner. I'm... We're running low on supplies. We'll have to make a run into town soon." I take a bite of my food and swallow without tasting it.

"We can go tomorrow." He takes another bite, then faces me. "About how...? Are you going to tell me what's going on in that pretty head of yours? At this point, secrets are more dangerous than being honest."

Sighing, I blow out a big breath. "I'm worried

about you. Your aura darkened some. What if some of the witches in town see us and can see that as well?"

His brows pinch together. "Our auras don't identify us as witches. Otherwise, we wouldn't have spent the last two years hiding what we were from each other. So, mine has changed. That's normal for anyone who's been through something that changes their belief in themself. Is it black now?"

"No. It's a darker red than it was before." Which, I guess, doesn't have to be a bad thing.

"That's not horrible. Someone will just think I'm having a bad day. I can't read auras, anyway. It's a pretty specific talent, like long-distance scrying." He finishes his dinner and sets his bowl aside. "I think there were maybe three witches at my school who could do it."

Laughing, I nod. "You're right. Until today, I'd never seen an aura, either. Think something in that room changed me? Other than the obvious."

"I don't know, but we'll figure it out." He scoots a little closer to me. I can't tell if he's doing it on purpose, or our connection is drawing him this way. "We do need to talk about what our next steps are."

"If today taught me anything, it's that I'm not prepared for this. I thought all the hate and rage I carried within me would be enough, but it was harder than I thought it would be. We also know that he has an extensive network of followers. That room could have held a coven three times the size of mine easily. Not to mention the amount of power he's harnessed there. It's enough to take me out without thinking twice about it."

Donovan reaches over and grabs my hand. "Us. You aren't alone, anymore. But I do agree. I underestimated everything about him. He's always been a cruel man. The depth of his desire for power is shown in how he collects human things like properties, businesses, and employees, who may actually be followers."

Pulling my hand free from his distracting touch, I stand and pace. My stomach turns over the watery mess I called dinner as I struggle to find a path that leads to us not dying. "Do we even have a chance?"

"Hey." Donovan stands and grabs my shoulders, which I didn't realize were shaking. "There's always a chance. We have several things working for us. He doesn't know we've stolen some of his power. In fact, he doesn't even know we're after him. We have the element of surprise on our side."

He's right, but it doesn't change the fact that we're incredibly outnumbered. Gregory also has years of experience on his side, and we're only just starting this magical journey.

I glance at the cave and realize we have one other thing on our side. Holding onto that little piece of hope, I grab Donovan's hand and pull him to the cave, snatching the lantern off the ground as I go.

"Are you going to lock me up again? I thought you trusted me now." The heartbreak in his voice pulls me up short, and I stop.

"Trust is a hard thing for me. We have a lot to talk through still, but I promise I'm working on it." With a small smile, I tug him to move again. "I don't plan on locking you up, though. We need each other, and it's comforting to not be alone again. I just want to show you something."

Donovan trots along beside me, and I flick on the lantern as we make our way to the back wall. There, I move the racks out of the way to reveal the entrance to the secret passage.

The dark walls surround us, and Donovan's face pinches as he looks around in confusion. I can't blame him. I did the same thing the first time I came back here.

"Stop looking and start seeing." It sounds odd coming from my lips, but he seems to understand what I mean.

Donovan closes his eyes and tilts his head back. His breathing evens out, and his body relaxes, the stiffness in his shoulders melting away.

"I can't sense anything." Disappointment flickers across his face.

"I didn't, either, in the beginning." But we don't have years for him to practice like I did, so I help him out.

Setting the lantern down, I reach for his hands. My magic swirls along my skin and connects with his, the two merging quickly like they were meant to be together.

His eyes shoot to me in wonder, but I'm not ready to deal with that, yet.

One step at a time.

His hands link tightly with mine, and he closes his eyes once more. I follow suit and push my earth magic out. The now-familiar hum of gold greets me, and I bask momentarily in its power, letting it wash over me and into Donovan. It makes me feel powerful, but I hold that thought in check.

"Gold." Wonder fills Donovan's voice. "Lots of it. I can't believe no one's taken it. I can't believe my father hasn't taken it."

"A gray witch coven discovered it years ago before they were wiped out by dark witches. I don't know if it was your father or someone else, but they hid their secret away." My heart breaks for Hattie and her family. I'm just glad she found a new home with the Barlows, then with me. She wasn't alone.

Donovan takes control and follows the line of gold as it weaves throughout the mountain. "There's so much. If we can harness it, we have an even better chance."

"That's why I wanted to show you this. I have this idea that I can put up extensions throughout the city to keep the flow going. Maybe we can even wrap the ring with the gold to amplify it as well? We have options now. I just need to stop being so negative and focus on the end game."

"We can do this. I know we can." He releases one of my hands and picks up the lantern. "We need to sleep, so we have clear heads and refreshed bodies because, tomorrow, we plan."

3

The next morning, we work out a plan to extend our ability to access the gold in the mountain from any point in town.

Donovan likes my idea about using gold disks as a way to hopscotch our magics back to the main vein but adds to that plan runes to hide the disks from anyone looking for or at them and to lock them to our personal magic. It won't do us any favors if we build up this giant power source, then allow someone to steal it from us.

I've been so focused on how to draw the power that I never once considered someone could take my link and use it against me. Which is a huge oversight on my part, considering Gregory's entire scheme is stealing the power from other witches and making it his own.

Donovan and I spend half the day drawing gold from the mountain, creating the disks, inscribing the spells onto them, and adding our blood to bind it to us. If there was a way to bind the entire mountain, we would, but we settle for adding masking spells to the cave and doubling up on the protection wards around the campsite.

By late afternoon, I'm tired and hungry, but we have a stack of small disks ready to be dispersed.

Donovan wipes the sweat from his brow. "I call a break."

Since my entire body aches like I was breaking rocks all day, I nod in agreement. While most of what we did was all mental, the cost of using magic for so long took a physical toll.

I sit on my log by the fire pit and eye the caldron. We have enough oats for another meal, but I really want something more substantial than that.

Donovan leaves me to run into the camper. We didn't sleep in there last night, but I showed him around so he knew where to find the essentials. He returns a moment wearing his coat and carrying mine. He also holds a cloth bag which he loads the small, gold disks into it, then stuffs it into his pocket.

"Come on." He thrusts my coat at me. "We're going for supplies."

"But...you called a break," I whine even as I shrug into my jacket. Now that I stopped moving, I'm cold, and since I didn't find the energy to build the fire back up, I welcome the added layer.

"I'll drive." He eyes my old truck. "That is, if that monster can really go anywhere."

"Hey, don't talk that way about my baby," I protest. "And who said you could drive my truck?"

"We're going into town, so it's best we don't take my SUV. Someone might recognize it." He jogs to the driver's side door and opens it. "Get in, slowpoke."

Grumbling, I trudge to the passenger side. I really don't have the energy to drive, anyway, and we *do* need supplies.

Donovan shakes his head as he finds the keys already in the ignition and turns them, the truck rumbling to life.

I pull on my seat belt. "What? It's not like anyone is going to come all the way out here to steal it."

"True." He backs the truck around his SUV, then follows the path down the mountain and to the main road.

I must doze off because I startle awake when a hand gently shakes my arm.

Groggy, I rub my eyes and look out the windshield and see a familiar diner. "What are we doing here?"

Donovan gives me an impish smile. "I'm hungry, and they have the best food in town."

Warmth floods through me as I remember all the times before that we came here as a couple. This is our place. Or, rather, it's Donovan and Evaine's place.

My smile dims. What are we now? Not dating. Not Donovan and Sabine. Despite falling in love, we've spent years hiding our true selves from each other. How do we start again, and should we even try? Our plan will end in us taking down Donovan's father, the man who murdered my entire family. What kind of foundation is that for happiness?

"Hey, it's just food." Donovan's hand falls from my arm. "We can go somewhere else if you want."

It's not just food, though, and we both know it.

With a deep breath, I turn my head to look at him and raise my brow. "Did being a gentleman get thrown out the window?"

A smile breaks across his face before he bolts out of the truck and runs around to my side.

Opening my door, he reaches up to steady me as I hop down. For a moment, only a hand's breadth of space separates our bodies, and it's just like old times. My pulse leaps, the cologne that still clings to his jacket filling my nose and bringing with it a sense of comfort. This is my safe place, my time when I can just be myself, without the weight of revenge hanging over me.

Donovan must feel it, too, because he swallows hard before he steps back and sweeps his arm toward the diner. "Our feast awaits."

My legs shake as I walk past him, and I tell myself it's the exhaustion and not because my heart won't stop racing.

The waitress who greets us at the door smiles. "Well, I haven't seen you two in a while! I thought you defected to one of the big chain restaurants."

Donovan throws his hand over his heart. "We would *never*!"

Laughing, she grabs two menus. "Table at the back?"

He grins. "You know it."

As she heads down the narrow aisle between tables and booths, Donovan's hand slips naturally to my back, and that shaky feeling increases. This all feels so natural, like nothing changed when our entire world turned upside down. The smell of greasy food floods my mind with memories linked to this place, trying to fold the part of me that was Evaine, that I separated just for Donovan, into the rest of. As much as I kept my time with Donovan separate from everything else, Evaine was still me, possibly the best part of me.

Donovan nudges me to the seat against the wall, the seat I always took so I could see the rest of the room and know if anyone was paying us special attention.

On autopilot, I take the menu the waitress holds out, though I already know what I'll order. Hash browns and eggs in the morning and burgers in the afternoon. It's what I always get, my two favorite things on the menu.

When she leaves, Donovan sets his menu aside, making it clear his mind is already set, too. "I've been craving a good burger and fries for days."

I stare at him with wide eyes. How can he look like everything's normal when my heart feels ready to burst?

The waitress returns with our waters, and I sit in silence while Donovan places my order, knowing without asking to leave off the onions and mayo, and that I want ranch for my fries.

As she leaves once more, I lean across the table. "What are you doing?"

His eyes widen. "Did you want something else? I can go grab her before she places the order."

"We're not a couple anymore," I hiss. "You shouldn't be ordering for me."

He gives me a steady look. "I agree, we're not a couple anymore."

Unreasonably hurt by his instant agreement, I sit back against my seat.

"We're more than a couple," he continues, his expression serious. "What we're doing... I don't know how it will end for us, but whatever the outcome, we'll end up there together. Life or death, we're bound. If we win—" He cuts off with a shake of his head. "*When* we win, the future will be open to us. No more darkness, no more threat. We'll be free. I hope that means we'll be free together. I choose *you*, however the cards land. You've been the only light in my life these past few years, and I refuse to believe that's changed just because we're finally being fully open with each other about who we are."

"And who are we?" I ask, my voice breaking on the words because I don't know anymore.

He reaches across the table to grasp my hands,

weaving our fingers together. "We're two broken people who have lost our families, had them ripped away by evil. And we're going to make sure this never happens again. We're going to right this wrong, then we'll figure out where we want to go after that. I have money in a trust fund. We can fix up the trailer and go anywhere we want. We'll make a new home of our choosing."

"I have a home." Unable to bear the hope in his eyes, I look down at our clasped hands. "Barlow Manor still stands. It's my heritage."

His fingers squeeze mine. "Is that what you want? To go back there?"

I consider that for a long time, long enough that our food arrives, and I pick at my fries as we eat in silence. Do I want to go back to Barlow Manor? It holds so many ghosts, so much horror. I don't know if I'll ever be able to wipe the phantoms of my slaughtered family from my mind. But it's so much more than their deaths. It was their lives, too. For generations, Barlow women raised their daughters and fostered other white witches, building a home of peace and, if not prosperity, at least comfort.

I can't be what my grandmother and mother were, though. I don't have it in me to fully embrace white magic. But I could breathe new life into the old house, build new traditions.

As the waitress clears away our empty plates and brings our strawberry milkshakes to go, I finally nod. “Yeah, once we’re through with this, I want to take back Barlow Manor.”

After restocking at the grocery store, we spend the rest of the day testing out our gold disks, seeing how far we can stretch before we lose contact with the mountain, then going in a little closer before burying the disks in the ground and putting more runes around them to ward off humans as well as animals. We don’t need crows spotting something shiny and flying away with it.

It takes into nightfall to spread the disks through the woods and city. By the time we’re through, a network of gold hums from all around us.

We settle down next to the fire, our feet near the flames as we share a blanket. Since we ate in town, we kept the flames low to conserve resources.

I struggle to relax, though, still worried that someone will manage to steal our network. “Are you sure other witches won’t feel this?”

How can they not, when the air vibrates with magic?

Donovan holds out his hand. "Give me your cuff."

My fingers curl possessively around the band of metal that circles my wrist before I reluctantly twist it off and pass it to him. Instantly, the magic vanishes from my senses, leaving me feeling blind, my senses dulled.

It makes me feel weaker, and my hand shakes as I snatch the band back. "Okay, point made. How did you get so good at masking magic?"

His lips thin. "It's one of the first things they taught us at school."

My figures rub over the gold cuff as I give him a curious glance. "What was it like?"

"The school?" At my nod, he frowns. "Like any other school, I guess. They started with the basics and moved up from there. There were some things I connected with and others I didn't. Like scrying."

"Ugh," I groan. "I always hated staring into those bowls of water."

He stares at me in surprise. "You used water?"

Now, it's my turn to frown. "Yes? What did you use?"

"Fire." He tilts his head to the side. "What about looking over distances?"

"Water," I say again. "Sometimes earth, though it's not as clear."

"Fire or mirrors, which I guess is like earth," he muses. "Huh. I thought the basics were all the same. Until, you know, the animal sacrifices started."

"We sacrificed animals, too." At his surprised look, I shrug. "We weren't vegetarians, and if a life was going to be taken, it would serve as much good as possible. Nothing was wasted."

He nods. "That makes sense. Pretty sure our rabbits didn't go into the stew pot, though."

I tip my head back against my log, my eyes focused on the stars overhead. It's a clear night, with a bright, waning crescent moon.

This time of month used to be about banishing negativity that built up over the month, sweeping the way clear for more positivity with the birth of the new moon. If only it were that easy to sweep away all of the negative. It will take more than simple, Moon Witch magic to defeat the Dark Witches.

"What are you thinking about?" Donovan whispers.

I roll my head to the side to find his eyes on the stars as well. "That we could use some luck right about now."

"Should we call four corners?" he asks.

My brows pinch together. “Don’t you need a ton of candles and a full coven for that?”

His lips curl into a smile. “Here’s where my training comes in handy. The classes I attended focused mostly on solo or partner.” Cold air rushes in as he throws off the blanket and stands. “I’ll be right back.”

I get to my feet as he hurries to the cave, and a moment later, the lantern flares to life. I watch him dig through the shelves. He returns with an emergency candle and our new canister of salt and uses his foot to clear off a part of the ground away from the fire pit. He sets his items down, then goes to the trailer, returning with two metal bowls and a cup filled with water.

Striding to his cleared piece of earth, he stabs the candle into the ground, compressing dirt around it to keep it upright. He then sets one of the bowls directly across from it and pours in a healthy amount of salt. Turning ninety degrees, he places the cup of water. Opposite that goes the second bowl, in which he places a tiny triangle of incense.

Straightening, he double-checks his preparation, then lights the candle and the incense before he beckons me over. “We’ll have to use your athame, since I don’t have one.”

About to protest that I don't have one, either, I realize he's talking about my scissors. I suppose they *are* my tool of power, though I can just hear my mother scoffing at using them in place of the sacred athame of our coven. My stomach tightens at the thought. We didn't find my coven's magic tools in Gregory's hidden lair. He must have a trophy case somewhere else, probably at his house, where he keeps the tools of power.

When this is over, I'll ask Donovan to help me search for them. He would know where best to search.

I pull the scissors from my belt as I join him in his circle. "Are you sure about this?"

He grins. "Trust me. This isn't the first time I've done this spell."

The worst that can happen is the spell doesn't work, so I nod in agreement.

Still smiling, he turns me to face the bowl of incense, then steps in close, his chest against my back. My pulse leaps in response as his arms wrap around me, his hands over mine on the scissors.

His warm breath flutters against my ear. "You know the words?"

"Yes," I groan, my whole body heating.

"Together then," he instructs. "Guardians of the watchtower of the East..."

"...we summon thee," I say in unison, calling on the powers of Air for inspiration.

We turn together to the South, moving clockwise, to call on the power of Fire to protect us. The flame glows brighter at our entreaty before we turn to the West, calling on Water for Wisdom.

Finally, we turn to North.

"Guardian of the watchtower of the North," we call, our voices ringing through the clearing. "Power of Mother Earth, we call on you for protection. Guard us from our enemies."

Together, we raise our arms over our heads, the point of the scissors aimed at the stars. "Bless this circle with your protection, and give us the strength to right what has been wronged. So mote it be."

Power surges through me, unlike any I've felt before. It fills me with warmth and light, washing away the strain of the day and leaving my pulse racing. My chest heaves as I struggle to breathe, then the power sweeps downward, the warmth turning to heat.

Donovan's hands leave mine on the blade to grip my shoulders and turn me in his arms.

The intensity of his gaze steals my breath all over again before his head dips, his lips claiming mine.

It feels like a binding, a sealing of our bond, and like coming home all rolled into one. Sagging against him, I wrap my arms around him and let myself go. No more thinking. Only the two of us exist, and for now, that's enough.

4

We spend the next three days camping in the woods near the cabin.

After hashing out various ideas, we finally decided we needed to know how big Gregory's coven is before we can truly plan an attack. A coven leader's power doesn't just come from themselves and their magic tools. It comes from those who swear allegiance to them. You don't have to be the most powerful member of a coven to lead one, you just have to be the person most trusted to wield the magic of everyone else for the good of the whole.

That's not to say that Gregory's *not* the most powerful. A man like him wouldn't trust anyone who could potentially overthrow him and take control. But we also know he doesn't work alone. Donovan already wrote down the names of everyone he was aware worked with his father, but that was his public coven, the one he showed off to other covens. There has to be a second, darker group with morals that align more directly with Gregory.

Since Donovan didn't know about his father's dark practices, he must have only met with them out here. For once, Macey seems to have told the truth. The guard would have woken up yesterday morning, knowing time passed. The question is whether he reported the possible leak right away or held off to save himself from reprimand.

Knowing how Gregory dealt with my family, I'm sure he held off. Allowing intruders to escape would come with a death sentence.

Which means, eventually, Gregory will come again with his coven, and we're banking on the darkest part of the moon cycle, the opposite end of the spectrum from when the Moon Witches are at their most powerful.

So, we pack up water and meal replacement bars, then trek into the woods from the opposite direction as the access road. I thank Hattie's training that we don't get lost. It's a slow process to reach the cabin, as Donovan and I work together to cast spells along the way, searching for the wards that alerted the guard to our presence the first time.

We find them at the edge of the treeline and decide not to mess with them. We can see the cabin from where we stopped, so there's no point in alerting the guard that we returned.

We take turns sleeping, huddled close together since we can't risk a fire, and on the third night, our efforts pay off.

As headlights break the darkness, I reach out to shake Donovan awake.

He blinks groggily. "Is it time to switch already?"

"Shh." I press a finger over his lips. "Someone's coming."

Alert now, he crawls out of the sleeping bag and crouches beside me. "Give me the binoculars. I might recognize them."

I pass them over, our fingers brushing in the process, and my pulse leaps. We didn't speak about what happened the night we summoned the four corners, but a closeness has existed since then that I can't bring myself to fight.

Donovan raises the binoculars to his eyes, then swears under his breath. "It's the guard."

My stomach tightens into a knot as I squint through the darkness. "Does it look like he's searching for us?"

Donovan watches for a minute before he shakes his head. "I think he's just checking to make sure the cabin's clear." He falls silent for another minute. "Now, he's speaking into a walkie-talkie. I think he's giving the go-ahead because he's heading for the outhouse."

Only the headlights from the SUV illuminate the clearing, but it's enough to see his dark figure walking toward the outhouse before coming right back.

A few minutes later, more cars pull into the clearing, their headlights flooding the empty cabin.

I count as people emerge, one, two, three... Nine in total, which is an odd number for a coven, unless three more are on their way. But that theory goes out the window when the last man heads for the cabin and climbs down into the underground room before the guard seals them inside.

"That was my dad," Donovan whispers. "The last one who went in."

A note of sad finality underlays his words. I think he was still holding out hope this was a big misunderstanding and that his dad wouldn't be one of the people who showed up.

Reaching out, I take his hand, and he clutches mine tight.

As the minutes tick by, we settle on the ground together, using the sleeping bag to keep warm.

"What do you think they're doing in there?" he asks.

I shake my head. "I don't know. Maybe plotting the next coven they'll obliterate?"

He shivers and leans closer, pressing his arm against mine. "How many do you think they've wiped out?"

"I don't know. At least two, between both of our moms." I look at him. "A dark coven wiped out my mentor's, too, years ago. I don't know if I want to hope it's the same group or not."

"Hope that it was them," he whispers. "If it's not, that means there's more out there."

"How are we going to deal with ten dark witches?" It's not a complete coven, but it's more than our numbers.

Donovan sits silently for a long time before he says, "I could go back to my dad's house. Tell him I've changed my mind about school. That I want to meet the coven as a full member."

It's a good idea, but it sends dread through me. "It's risky. He'll wonder where you've been."

"He knows I had a girlfriend in town who wasn't one of us." He stares at the cabin, his profile grim. "I can tell him we broke up. That I realized once it was no longer long distance that we were too different."

"What will you do once you meet the rest of the coven?" Fear makes my throat tight. Now that we're unofficially back together, I don't want to lose him again.

He turns his head to stare down at me, his face masked in shadows. "Kill them all."

The suggestion doesn't shock me so much as Donovan being the one to do it. "How?"

"Poison?" he offers. "Or a spell? Something they won't detect until it's too late."

"How would you do it?" I ask, trying to ignore the fact we're talking about killing nine people, ten if we're lucky enough to get his dad in the process.

"I've sat in on some of the welcoming ceremonies when they bring in a new member." He turns his attention back to the cabin. "They pass around a chalice. It's supposed to represent the blood of the coven. Dad always told me it was really wine, but now, I'm not so sure. If I can slip something into it, they'd all drink it willingly. Then, we'd just have to wait for it to take effect."

That could work, so long as his dad doesn't suspect Donovan of defecting. "I think there's a spell like that in the dark grimoire. We can look when we get back to camp."

Something catches Donovan's attention at the cabin, and he lifts the binoculars back to his eyes. "I think they're coming back out."

In the headlights from the SUV, I see the guard striding back to the outhouse, and a moment later, the coven members crawl out from beneath the cabin. Their dark shapes remind me of cockroaches. I hope they're not as hard to kill.

As cars begin to pull away from the cabin, I frown. "There were only nine."

Donovan looks down at me. "What?"

"Ten went down, but only nine came up." I grab the binoculars from him and lift them to my eyes.

Instead of closing the hidden passageway back up as I expect, the guard climbs down into the depths. Minutes tick by, then a strange, bulbous white shape appears, wavering back and forth out of the hole like a giant worm. Then, shoulders appear before the entire torso heaves upward and flops onto the ground.

Queasy, I lower the binoculars. "The tenth was a sacrifice."

Donovan snatches the binoculars from my slack fingers to look for himself as my stomach twists with nausea. We watched that person go willingly into the subterranean room. What if they thought they were going to be brought into the secret coven? What if they drank from the goblet the way Donovan described only to find themselves the sacrificial goat?

What if the same happens to Donovan?

Reaching out, I clutch his hand. "You can't go back. I don't trust your father not to kill you."

"It'll be okay." But the shake in his voice shows he doesn't believe it. "He won't hurt me until he has another heir."

"How do we know he doesn't already?" I demand. "For all we know, he has kids stashed all around the country."

Donovan shakes his head. "He wouldn't do that."

"You can't know that," I insist.

"When he gave me the talk about the birds and the bees, he told me that every child steals some of your magic." He reaches out and cups my face. "I know he doesn't have a dozen kids because he's too hungry for power to lose magic that way. I'm safe so long as I don't give him a reason to do away with me."

I still don't like it. I've spent so many years planning this revenge on my own that it's hard to step back and let someone else take the risk. But it's the best option we've come up with so far.

Taking a deep breath, I nod in acceptance.

Donovan bends to press a kiss to my forehead. "I'll be safe. I promise. And I'll message every day."

I nod again, and we sit in silence as we watch the guard dig a hole behind the outhouse and bury the body before he leaves.

Once his headlights fade, we risk using the lantern we brought to pack up our gear and return to our campsite. No way are we staying here overnight with a dead body so close by.

The trek back through the woods goes faster than our trek in, since we no longer have to worry about setting off possible wards, and we make it back to where we hid my truck before two in the morning.

As we drive back to the campsite, the roads are empty of other cars, and without discussing it first, we go into the camper and lock the door.

It's not much to keep intruders out, but neither of us wants to sleep out in the open tonight.

Quietly, we get ready for bed, then crawl beneath the covers. There's not much room, but I'm used to cramped spaces after years of living out here. When

Donovan pulls me into his arms, I go willingly, not wanting to be separated before we have to be.

I wrap my arm tight around his waist, our legs tangling together beneath the covers. With my head on his chest, I listen to the steady thump of his heart and his even breaths until dawn brightens the windows, and I finally allow my eyes to close.

When I finally wake again, the sun floods the camper with light and Donovan's spot on the bed is empty. When I sweep my hand over the indent left by his body, the sheets are cool, so it wasn't him leaving that woke me.

My head feels fuzzy as I swing my legs out of bed and stand. While I slept, my dreams were plagued with images of crows feasting on skulls. I haven't had nightmares like that in a while, and I'm not happy to have them return. I need a clear head right now, not restless nights.

When I push open the door to the camper, the smell of wood smoke and coffee greet me.

"Lunch is almost ready," Donovan calls as I stumble down the step to the ground.

Stumbling over to join him, I give a half coherent

grunt, which he laughs at before pressing a hot mug into my outreached hand.

As I sip, I watch him add cinnamon and blueberries to bowls of porridge, and my stomach rumbles with demand. I can't believe I'm hungry after what we witnessed last night, but I suppose horror doesn't negate the need for food.

We eat in companionable silence, and the fog from my mind clears with every bite until I feel alert enough to function like a real human being instead of a zombie.

Donovan grins as he tops off my coffee cup. "There's my sunshine. Feeling better now?"

Heat creeps up my cheeks. "Shut up."

He fidgets while I sip my second cup, but he waits patiently until I set my empty cup aside. Then, he just stares at me expectantly.

Pursing my lips, I stand and stride back to the trailer to grab the dark grimoire from its current resting place on the small dining table. Why it decided to camp out there, I have no idea. I left it under the seat in Donovan's SUV.

I return to the fire pit, sit beside Donovan, and rest the book on my lap. "You really think this is the only way?"

His leg presses against mine. "Can you come up with a better solution?"

Since I can't, I focus on the grimoire. "Show us a spell to take out a lot of people."

5

My eyes cross. We've been researching different spells and potions all day. At this point, we've eliminated all the spells because they require some sort of rune to be used as a trigger. Most of these witches, especially his dad, would notice a rune drawn on the cup, assuming Donovan could even find the time or right instrument to do it.

"We don't have to do this tomorrow, you know." Donovan shuts the dark grimoire and pulls me against his side so my head rests on his shoulder.

"I know. It's hard, though. This has been all—well, mostly all—that I've thought about for the last two years. I just want to finish it and move on, whatever that means." I snuggle closer, absorbing his warmth and support.

He links his fingers through mine. "When you weren't thinking about this, what were you thinking about?"

"You. A life away from magic, pain, and heartache. I was so bad at magic that I couldn't do anything but doubt myself. Life would be simpler if I had just moved on."

"We've talked about this. We can still walk away. Hide somewhere."

I shake my head, my thoughts confused because, now that we're back together, that vision is front and center again. "As much as I'd love to walk away, I don't think either of us would actually be able to move on. This would always be hanging over us."

His thumb skims over the back of my hand, the brief touch grounding me. "It would, but I'd do it for you, for us."

Shifting, I rest my hand on his chest and stare into his green eyes. "You're the only reason I'd pull back now. My stomach is in knots thinking about you going back to him, putting yourself in danger. And returning to your original statement, I think we do have to do this now. Either that or switch our plans. The longer we wait, the less plausible your reason for going back is. That just puts you in more danger." Tears well up, and I let them spill over. "I can't lose you, too."

Donovan cups my face and kisses the tears away. "You aren't going to lose me." His lips tenderly brush mine, then he pulls me closer. "It's late, we can't read anything else in the dark, and if we do find something, we won't be able to prepare it now, anyway. Sleep, my warrior."

After sniffing back the rest of my tears, I finally fall into a restless sleep.

The morning rays of the sun warm my face, but I'm not ready to wake. Today's the day... if we can find some potions that will work.

Donovan stirs, but he doesn't make a move to get up, either, the weight of today falling on both of us.

We lie there for another hour, neither of us moving, neither of us sleeping. Part of me wants to reach out, grab the dark grimoire, and research more, but the other part of me is still scared that I could lose Donovan. Just when I thought I was alone, he walked back into my life. But fate played us a cruel hand by not letting us relax and enjoy that reunion. We have to work for it.

With that last thought, I run my nose across the stubble on Donovan's jaw, kiss the corner of his mouth, then pop up before I stay there and explore more. The only thing keeping me together is the idea that we'll get through this, but if I allow my heart to guide me, we'll lose from the distraction.

After we both clean up, I fix breakfast while Donovan makes coffee. We work together side-by-side like we've been doing this for years.

"Okay. Let's do this." I sit and sip some of the coffee. Once I've had a little bit of caffeine, I pull the dark grimoire onto my lap. "Do we want to incapacitate or kill them?"

We debated this last night, but with such a heavy decision and a night's sleep, I want to discuss it again.

Donovan runs his hands through his brown hair. It's gotten longer on top, and the look is more relaxed than some of the cuts he's had in the past. "I don't want to be my dad, but I also don't trust that one of them won't step up. Look at Macey. She'd immediately take up my dad's cause. She's that power-hungry."

"Yep. If I hadn't locked her down, she'd have come after me. She's dangerous," I agree.

"Some of the people around my dad have been there as long as I can remember. If Macey was like that after only a couple years, think about what those other men and women will be like."

"I wish we could bind their magic, but that takes a triad, and we only have the two of us." Maggie hops onto my lap, somehow managing to push the grimoire aside even though the tome outweighs her.

"What if we can?" Donovan picks up the white cat and cuddles her to his chest.

I glare at her betrayal. If I tried that with her, she'd scratch my eyes out.

"How?" Skepticism clouds my voice.

"I'm not sure. What if we use their magic as the third? The triad is meant for one of us to feed magic to the others. If we use their magic as the third with one of us creating the binding, then we should have the power to do it." Donovan sits up taller and scratches Maggie's neck, proud of himself for coming up with a solution.

Biting my lip, I worry that this is just wishful thinking. "I'm not an expert on triad magic. All of my studies with Hattie were around individual magic because, deep down, we knew, in the end, it would just be me fighting. Hattie was getting too old to do more than instruct me."

"I think it can work, but let's hold it in reserve while we research other options. I don't want to go around killing people, but we know at least the nine who were there last night aren't innocents. They let someone be sacrificed. We have to do something to stop them before more people die by their hand." Donovan plays with his mother's ring, which now hangs on a chain around his neck.

I reach over and grasp his other hand. "We aren't going to let them hurt anyone else."

Chanting that to myself, I turn the page of the grimoire and read the next potion. I work out my worry and negativity as I search. An important part of this will be our attitudes going into it, so I have to be firm in my resolve that what we decide will not only work but is the right and only way to handle the dark coven.

But page after page holds no help. When I ask the grimoire, death and destruction are the only spells that come up.

"Oooh. What about this?" I bounce the book on my legs, finally finding something that may work. "This potion incapacitates the drinker, both body and magic, for an hour. That would give us time to cast some of the rune spells. Trying to force a second potion into someone would be hard, and mixing potions could be deadly."

Donovan leans over my shoulder and reads the potion details. "And look, there's a sister potion which counters the effects."

"That would be good, you can take that before you drink from the cup." Some of the heaviness on my chest releases.

"Well..." Donovan looks away from me, and the relief I felt a moment ago is slapped away. "I was thinking I would transport the potion in my blood, cutting my finger to release the potion into the cup. I read a host spell in the grimoire. I wouldn't be affected by the potion in my blood steam—"

"Until you drank it like everyone else." I shake my head. "There has to be a better way."

"I might be able to take the antidote along with it. Since I would be acting as the host, it shouldn't react to anything in my blood."

"We don't know that, though, and don't have time to test it." I start to look for a different spell, but Donovan's hand stops me from turning the page.

"If we're going to do this with me as the bait, we don't have other options. The worst that could happen is I pass out with everyone else, and you have to come in and rescue me."

"Or the antidote negates the potion, and you're sucked into some weird, dark circle that I can't break you out of." Shivers course through me. I need to focus on positive outcomes.

Donovan kisses my temple. "Let's just run away."

Melting against his side, I play with that option. Life could be so much easier if we leave. We could even find a small white or gray coven to join, somewhere in another state. We could build our own life somewhere. We don't need a big coven to do magic, Hattie and I proved that. A small cabin in the middle of nowhere. Gardens and animals could be our focus, just doing what we have to do to get by.

Then, I remember who Donovan's dad is. Gregory will never willingly let his heir go. He'll track us down no matter how many protection spells we use. Our children would never be safe from their grandfather, because as soon as we had a son, Gregory would be there to steal him away.

My resolve firms once more. "No. We have to do this. There are no other viable options because Gregory will be there every step of the way. Even if we could look past what we know he'd do to other witches, what he's done to our families, he'll never let you go that easily. We'd always be looking over our shoulder, wondering if he's in the shadows waiting for us to make a wrong move so he can find you and tear us apart."

Donovan rests his forehead on mine. "I'm willing to take that chance for you. I just want us to be happy."

"What about the chance for our children?" I stumble over that word because we haven't talked about a real future. Even when we were dating, the idea of a future wasn't brought up. We lived in the now, which is why we never got around to talking about our families.

"I'd never let him touch you, our children, or our grandchildren." Steel fills his voice, and I believe he means everything word.

"I know. I wouldn't, either, which is why I want to stop him now. I don't want our children to have to constantly be on the lookout or in fear for their lives." I realize now that this won't end without the death of Gregory Crawford.

Donovan takes the dark grimoire from me and rereads the potion. "Let's start this."

6

"So, we know we're going to use the potion to incapacitate everyone. Then what?" While this is our only option, I want each step planned out. We can't afford any mistakes.

"Once everyone is down, we set a circle around them and siphon their magic out, using it, the gold, and my family's magic to bind them. You can be the conduit for the gold while I'm the conduit for my family's magic," Donovan recites.

"But how will I know you're ready for me to come in?" Each element has to be precise. It's the only way to defeat, not just a dark coven, but a man as powerful as Gregory.

Donovan paces away from me. Even though we

know what we want to do, we haven't started talking through how to actually execute it. This may be our biggest hurdle.

"I can signal you," he says.

"How?"

"Uhm." He purses his lips at me. "Is there a spell for you to hear what I'm saying?"

"Probably, but I bet yo—Gregory," I revise quickly. I'm trying to avoid calling him Donovan's dad. As much as he says he's ready for this, I can't imagine what it will be like face-to-face, so even the smallest of separation could help, "has wards up to stop things like that. We need something else."

"What about going the human route?" he asks.

My brows pinch. "What do you mean?"

"We can get listening devices. He may take my phone away, or ban electronics from being in the room with us, but I've never seen him do a sweep for bugs before. He's too into magic for anything as mundane as a human invention to mess up his plans."

I laugh for the first time in a while. "It would be funny to take him down without an ounce of magic, not that I think that's possible unless one or both of us become expert marksmen in the next twenty-four hours. Using listening devices is a good start, though."

Donovan runs inside and grabs a piece of paper and a pencil. "I'll start making a list, so we don't forget or miss anything."

"Okay, so the plan is for you to go home and talk to Gregory..."

"Yes. I'll tell him I've done some soul searching over the last couple of days. I wasn't sure what I wanted from my life, which is part of the reason I came back. After I realized my girlfriend here moved on, there was nothing more holding me back from finishing my education," he recites.

The story's plausible. From my limited interaction with teens my age and the books I've read, they tend to hesitate to commit to anything too early in life.

"At this point, we're going to assume that he wants to induct you into his dark coven, but what if he doesn't? What's the next move?" I ask.

"This is the trickiest part, I think, because I can't just up and ask to be included in his secret coven. He'd know something was up. I was thinking I'd ask him to tutor me, since I'll have missed out on a semester. I can play up his ego, which will soften him to my requests." Donovan rolls his eyes. From what he's told me, Gregory is the most self-centered person on the planet. An ego boost will probably go a long way.

"So, if we have to go that route, we could be waiting for days, weeks, or even months." This is where I have to force that positivity bubble around myself. I can't imagine Donovan being in that house for months on end with no guarantee that I can see or talk to him during that time.

He cups my cheek and uses the pad of his thumb to brush away a tear. "I won't let that happen. I'll be the best student he's ever had. With the help of the white magic we're stealing from him, I'll be able to advance quickly. He'll want me to learn as much as possible at that point."

"Okay," I say hesitantly. "So, now we're at the ceremony. We can't assume it will happen at the cabin. What if he has another site that we don't know about?"

"This part may be tricky, too."

"There isn't a part of this plan that isn't tricky." A dry laugh escapes me. I'm not cut out for spy stuff. "We just need to understand the risks so we can mitigate them where possible."

"You're going to have to be constantly listening to catch something."

My eyes widen, and fear strikes at my chest. "This is such a bad idea. What if he comes to get you in the middle of the night, and I'm sleeping, or the earpiece needs to be charged? We don't even know if I can get a signal out here."

"We'll add it as an app on your phone. We know you get reception out here, so it will work."

"And if my phone dies? It's not like I've got a lot of power source options out here." As hard as I try to push back all the negativity, the pressure continues to build.

"I'll buy a generator. You forget that I have money, money my dad doesn't have access to. A generator is a good investment even if we end up running away in the end." He raises his brows at me.

I wave my hand in the air. "Fine. We'll need to stock up on fuel, too. I won't have this phone die. I'm probably going to have to come up with a spell to stay awake for days on end or exhaustion will knock me out."

"Sleep during the day. He keeps a strict work schedule to keep up appearances. I don't expect anything to happen at that time."

"But it could—"

"It's unlikely, so please get some sleep," he cuts in,

his expression serious. "You're going to need your strength when the time comes."

He pulls me down next to him as we finish going over every detail, then patiently goes over it again. I could kiss him for that. He knows I need this plan memorized to be able to follow through. This was so much easier when I was the only one putting my life on the line.

By the time we run through the plan a third time and our list of supplies is done, it's comprehensive, and we'll work separately to make it faster to collect everything.

We stop and eat dinner. Time slipped by quickly as we worked through the plan. My mind is exhausted, but my body is wired with nervous energy.

"Do you want to get some sleep?" Donovan asks as he sets the cleaned cauldron near the fire. "We can get up early and start again."

"I know I need to, but I doubt I can. Do you think every night will be like this?" I scoot over so Donovan has room to snuggle in next to me.

Maggie tries to crawl between us, but Donovan's

body is pressed up against mine, so she ends up sitting on his legs instead

"I'm going to miss this, miss you. I have no doubt both of us will struggle with sleep." Donovan flips to his side as he pulls me closer. "Sleep while I can still hold you. Together, we can accomplish anything."

Resting my head on his shoulder, I close my eyes, willing sleep to come. "Goodnight."

Vivid dreams fill my mind as a circle of skulls surround a pair of doves. Ravens as black as a moonless night perch on each of the skulls, and blue fire dances around all of them. Hisses and pops fill the air as the ravens cry out.

"Sabine," Donovan calls my name and shakes my shoulder. "Sabine, wake up. You're having a nightmare."

I bolt upright and rub my eyes. The sun barely peeks over the horizon, and long shadows cast the campsite into darkness. I wonder briefly if I'm still asleep, but Donovan's hand on my back eases that worry away. It was just a dream.

"Sorry. I have some crazy dreams sometimes."

Donovan rubs small circles on my back. “Maybe you’re a Seer. That’s a strong, white magic.”

“Not that I know of, but I don’t know much about my dad’s side of the family, either. I shouldn’t have inherited his magic, but we know that my magic was messed up before birth, so anything is possible.” It’s not common for witches in the Barlow family to be close to their fathers. I never understood that, but Mom and Grandmother were never bothered by it. After dating Donovan, I can’t imagine being alone like they were. “Even if I’m a Seer, I have no idea what any of it means.”

“I never understood those things, either. Fate is never set. We have choices along the way that can upset the balance.” Donovan stands, brushes his jeans off, then helps me up.

I squeeze his hand before I let it go. “I always looked at it as the thing most likely to happen based on decisions already made. It can change, but if those plans work out, that vision is what is likely to happen. But... since my dreams are always symbolic in nature, it could lead to anything.”

Grabbing our list, I pick up the lantern, and we make our way to the cave. We should have all the ingredients for the potions, but I haven’t taken an inventory in a while. Also, some things lose potency if left unused for too long.

Inside, I pass the list and lantern to Donovan. He starts reading off ingredients, and I place them in a small basket Hattie kept in here for her *shopping*, as she liked to call it.

"We're missing a few things. Let's double-check the items we do have to make sure I didn't miss any. Bone?" Donovan asks.

"Got it."

"Oregano?"

"Yep."

"Rose petal?"

"Check."

"We have campfire ash out there," he says to himself. "Feverfew?"

"Yep."

"Nettles?"

"We have some, but they're old," I tell him.

"Okay. What about amethyst?" he asks.

There's none here, but I know where there is some. My throat closes at the idea of digging into Henry's collection. He's an innocent in all of this. Dragging him into it makes me nauseous.

Donovan's hand lands on my shoulder. "Hey. What's going on?"

"Nothing." I shake off the queasiness. "I know where we can get amethyst."

"But?"

"No buts."

He turns me toward him and cups my cheeks. "I know you well enough to know a *but* when I see one. Talk to me."

"My brother, Henry, collected rocks, gems, and minerals. There's an amethyst in his collection," I explain with a broken sob.

"No. We don't need to use that. We're going to have to go into town anyway to pick up the generator and listening devices. We can stop by a jewelry store to get one or one of those touristy places and buy a geode. There's no reason to break up your brother's collection."

Throwing my arms around Donovan's neck, I nearly knock us over as I kiss his neck. "Thank you, thank you."

He pulls me close and kisses my temple. "Anything for you."

We stand like that for another minute. Once he sets me back on my feet and steadies me, he goes back to the list. "Last thing on here is skullcap."

"We don't have that. It's rare and dangerous if used in the wrong way." Herbology was one of the few classes I paid attention to growing up because my grandmother loved it so much. She shared that love with us each lesson.

"Great." Donovan sets the list in the basket, then picks it up. "That means it's not something we can pick up in town."

"Nope, but I know where to get some." I follow Donovan out of the cave.

"That's good. Where?"

"Back at Barlow Manor," I answer.

"No. Absolutely not." Donovan sets the basket down by the lantern and waves his hands at me. "You were almost caught there twice."

"I wasn't caught, though. I'll be okay."

"We'll go together," he says.

"No. We don't have time for all of that. We need to split up, especially if you have to go into the big city to get to a good electronics store. I don't think Manberry will have what you're looking for. We need to gather all our supplies today, so splitting up is our best option."

He runs his fingers through his brown hair, turning it into an unruly mess. "I don't like it."

"I don't like it, either," I agree. "I don't like that you're going to have to go back to that house, with *him*, and without me, but we know it's for the best. I know what I'm going for, so I'll be in and out quickly. I can also gather the stinging nettles while I'm there. I'm an expert at collecting those."

I can't help but let out a sad laugh. That was my number one punishment when I broke the rules. It was also the last directive I was given by my mom before she was killed. I was out collecting nettles while my family died.

"Fine, let's get this over with. I want to start the rest of my life with you." He pulls me into a rough kiss, all the anger and fear of being separated crashing between us.

The kiss slowly settles into a passion that I've missed. The pure joy of being together cascades through me and builds my confidence that we can get through the coming battle. Our love is meant to be, and defeating Gregory will be the next step in seeing it happen.

"We'll meet back here in two hours. If you aren't going to make it because you have to go into the big city, text me. Okay?" I ask.

He's in as much danger as I am if anyone sees him in town. He hasn't gone back to his father, yet, so who knows what his people think is going on.

"Two hours. You text me when you get back to the campsite, if you return before me." He thinks for a second. "In fact, text me when you reach the manor."

"Don't read any of my texts while you're driving!" I scold him.

"I won't. I'll make it into town before you reach the manor, so I'll be walking around." He kisses my nose, then pecks me on my swollen lips. If he kissed me like he did a second ago, we may not leave here today.

We separate and walk to our vehicles. He lets me leave first, then follows me as far as the turn-off toward Manberry. Watching his taillights disappear in my rearview mirror makes a lump form in my throat, but I swallow it down and drive toward the back entrance.

The path out this way is still untouched, so as long as I stop here, no one will realize that a second drive cuts through here. It probably isn't the safest of moves, but I don't want to take the time to cut through the forest. That takes more time and energy, and I want to make sure I'm back before Donovan is.

I park behind the old garage, grateful to see it still stands.

As soon as I'm out of the truck, I pull a string from my pocket and weave the pattern between my fingers to search for traps and wards. I walk with it in front of me, senses on high alert. Like the last couple of visits back here, the way is clear, but I still stick to the tree-covered paths to help hide my movement.

After making a circuit around the building to ensure no cars are parked here, I race across the garden, open the back door, and head into the house. Once inside, I run to the library.

Everything looks the same as when I last came here. Moving to the hidden entrance to the vault, I open it.

Darkness greets me, which feels fitting for what the vault hides. I forgot to bring the lantern, so I use my phone to light the way. Since I charged it on the drive over, using the light won't eat into my battery life.

At the bottom of the steps, I head toward the wall where the forbidden ingredients are housed. They aren't really forbidden, but we were lectured often about the dangers they pose. At some point, I should have cleared these stores out and moved them to the mountain, but I didn't want to spend more time here than necessary.

The skullcap is where I expect to find it, and I grab the entire jar. I don't have anything to carry it in, and there's no reason to leave any behind.

Leaving the vault, I close and hide the door once more, then head back outside.

I forgot to bring gloves, so collecting the nettles will be painful, but that will only hurry me along. Afraid I'll drop the precious jar as I pick my way through the woods, I carefully set it at the outer corner of the garden. I waffle for a moment before adding my phone, too. If I lose it while fighting through the overgrowth, it will add unnecessary time to find it again. With them safely hidden, I cut through the weeds and other overgrowth to reach the best patch of nettles.

Pulling my shirt from my waistband, I drape it over my thighs as I crouch and pull my scissors in one hand. I clip the stems haphazardly, avoiding the stinging barbs as much as possible. I can just hear my grandma's lecture in my mind, but I'm not worried about regrowth at this point. I just need enough for the spell.

When I have several pieces collected in the hem of my shirt, I stand and head back out of the woods. It reminds me of the last time I made this trek and the horror that awaited me at the house. I struggle to push the memory aside as I step out of the woods, then freeze.

Past and present merge as I come face to face

with an older version of Donovan. My hands fall to my sides, the scissors and nettles dropping to the ground.

Gregory's green eyes, so much like Donovan's, pin me in place. "Well, well, well. Look what we have here."

7

Fear freezes me in place for a moment as I hear the blood rushing through my veins and my family's screams echoing from the past. Then, training kicks in, and I dodge to the left, diving into the tall weeds as I yank the string from my pocket and weave my way into invisibility.

"Do you really think that white magic will keep you hidden?" Gregory says as he pushes through the brush. "The illusive Barlow daughter has finally come creeping back home. But what were you looking for?"

My heart pounds as I watch him bend and pick up a nettle between his thumb and forefinger. Adrenaline makes me shaky as I crawl farther away from him, slow and awkward on my elbows as I keep the string taut between my fingers.

I need fire or water. Why did Hattie put so much focus on elements that aren't readily at hand? Sleep. Can I put him to sleep? No, I'll never get that close.

"Now, what could you possibly have needed nettles for?" His voice comes from farther away. "Incense, perhaps? Are you feeling sad after I murdered your mommy? How long did you cry? Or maybe you need it for medicine? These weeds won't cure what ails you. It's too bad you're a Moon witch. If you were one of *my* disciples, I'd show you how to bring your family back."

Temptation hooks into my soul. To see my mom and Henry again, or even Hattie. To have any of my family back… But, no, there's nothing of them to bring back. Their magic passed into me, and no amount of wishful thinking can breathe life into them once more.

"Was it you at the cabin?" he asks, his voice growing more distant. "Are you the reason Macey vanished?"

I still, the blood freezing in my veins. If he guessed that, then will he guess about Donovan, too?

"She was a silly girl," he continues. "So desperate to fit in. She told me about your family, you know.

About how they kicked her out for being too bad. She was the one who suggested I come for a visit. Did you kill her?"

Grass crunches from nearby, and my head jerks up just as a hand fists in the back of my jacket.

"There you are, little mouse." Gregory yanks me up, kicking and screaming, and he rips the string from my fingers. "Trevor told me about your trick with string. Now, *there* was a witch with ambition. Too bad about his death. I couldn't even harvest his heart because *someone* stabbed right through it." His cold eyes stare into mine, and I take back my initial thought. They're nothing like Donovan's. "Sabine, right? That's your name? I'm going to enjoy taking your heart."

Desperate, my hand darts toward his forehead, but he dodges easily, laughing at my attempt to put him to sleep.

I reach for my scissors, but my belt is empty, my scissors lost somewhere in the weeds. Fear slices through me, and I kick out, my boot landing solid against his leg before he lifts a fist and pain explodes across my temple, followed by darkness.

When I wake up, my head throbs with pain, but I embrace the feeling since I didn't think I'd wake at all.

Groggy, I look around at my surroundings. Nothing looks familiar, and fear slides through me once more. Wherever Gregory took me, it wasn't to the cabin, which means Donovan arriving to save me went from hopeful to near impossible. I don't even have my phone to call for help, not that I know where I am, anyway.

The small room holds a couple lockers across from where I lie, and the white tile floor chills my skin. Dusky light seeps in through a window high on the wall, well out of reach. Dusk or dawn? How long was I out? Surely not a full day. The smell of chlorine fills the air, so there must be a pool nearby. Did Donovan's house have a pool? Would his father bring me back to his private residence? But why? Why not just cut out my heart on the spot? Or was he not prepared for that kind of spell when he found me? Was he just there on business? He *was* planning to demolish my ancestral home to build a resort. Was it just dumb luck that our paths crossed?

Groaning, I force myself into a sitting position. He bound my hands behind my back, and my shoulders ache from the strain. A rope winds around my ankles, too, with a lead attached to the leg of a bench screwed into the floor.

He didn't gag me, though, and I focus on the ropes as I whisper a spell to unravel the knot.

Nothing happens.

Focusing through the pain in my head, I try again. It's a basic spell that any witch can perform, but the magic inside me stays dormant. The rope stays tied.

My focus shifts back to the room, searching for the spells that must be in place to prevent me from using magic. I used a similar spell when I caught Macey, and I spot the runes carved into the wooden beams along the ceiling. There are probably more within the walls and under the floor. This place was designed to hold witches.

The fact Gregory put me in storage instead of killing me sends a shiver down my spine. All of the careful planning Donovan and I did, and none of it revolved around what to do if *I* was captured. He was supposed to be the one stepping into the lion's den, not me. I fought his plan every step of the way before I caved and tried to cover every angle of what could go wrong.

Stupid, stupid, stupid. Why did I let myself believe someone else could take the burden of my revenge? This was always going to be me alone. That's what Hattie trained me for, and her sharp voice fills my mind now, demanding I stop wallowing and start dealing.

I bang my head against the wall, escalating my headache to new heights. There's no time to berate myself for the mistakes I made. This is where I'm at now, so what's my next step?

Scooting across the tiles, I study the metal leg my feet are bound to. In the dim light, it looks like a basic, straight piece of metal, with heavy bolts securing it to the floor. Rather cheap design. Not something I'd expect from a man of Gregory's wealth. But maybe he only puts the people he plans to kill here, and a nicer pool house for his guests exists somewhere nearby.

I scoot back across the floor, painfully wedging the bench leg between my bound ankles until the rough edge digs into the rope. Stomach tensing, I lift and lower my legs in a sawing motion while pushing forward.

It takes a long time for the first rope to snap, long enough for the light to completely fade from the room and for my legs to grow tired with exhaustion. But all of Hattie's drills pay off as the binding around my legs loosens. Yanking my legs back and forth, I get the rope unraveled enough to pull my right foot free, then shake my left until the rope falls completely off.

For a moment, I lie on the floor, gasping in deep breaths before I force myself upright and turn to start on the rope around my wrists.

Now that night has fallen, my pulse races faster with the need to get out of here. How long before Gregory gathers his coven? How long before they come to take my heart? Every second that passes feels like a nail in my coffin, and I almost sob with relief when the rope on my wrists gives.

Pain floods down from my shoulders to my fingertips as blood rushes back in to fill my limbs. I clutch my hands to my chest as I stumble to my feet and over to the lockers against the wall.

It takes effort to curl my numb fingers around the first latch, and the door remains fixed in place for a moment before my special knack pushes the lock over. Thank the gods that the magic surrounding this room didn't strip me of the gift that not even my family's bindings could strip away.

The first locker holds foam pads and pool noodles that spring out at me as soon as the door opens. I jump back, stifling a scream, before I move on to the next. Here I find a volleyball and a net. I pluck at the threads until I pull one free that's long enough to weave between my fingers. The next locker holds snorkelers and goggles. I grab a pair of goggles, stretching them between my hands to test their strength. As far as weapons go, they're not ideal, but they're all I have.

A quick search of the room reveals nothing else of use, so I tiptoe to the door and press my ear against the sold surface. Muffled shuffling comes from the other end. A guard. Of course, Gregory wouldn't leave me completely unattended while he prepped.

With the goggles in one hand, I reach for the doorknob with the other.

As soon as the lock turns, I yank the door open and fling my arm up.

The goggles smack the startled guard in the face as he whirls, nailing him in the eyes. I continue forward, my training with Hattie brings my arm in a downward swing right between his legs. He buckles as I spin, and my elbow connects with the side of his head. He falls sideways, half landing in the open doorway, and I slam my palm onto his forehead, pushing his mind into sleep.

My heart races, my breaths coming in fast pants as I kneel in the hallway in shock, telling my body to get moving again. It all happened so fast my mind is still catching up. Why couldn't it have been like this when I faced Gregory earlier? Because he was the one to surprise me.

Standing on shaky legs, I drag the guard into the prison room, then rifle through his pockets. All I find is a cell phone, and I press his finger against the reader to unlock it before quickly dialing Donovan's number.

It rings on the other end before shuffling me to voicemail.

"Donovan, this is Evie, I think I'm in your pool house. Don't come. I think your dad suspects. I've escaped and am coming back to you," I whisper quickly before I hang up, make sure the phone is on silent, then stuff it into my pocket.

Tiptoeing out of the pool house, I lock the door behind me and sneak down the stone pathway toward a glowing, blue light. The smell of chlorine intensifies, and I duck behind some ornamental bushes to peer through the gaps in the leaves. Definitely Donovan's house. I recognize the house from the one time I visited. Across the large pool, a large pool house full of windows casts sunny yellow light onto the tiled slates, and figures move around within.

That must be one of the gatherings Donovan spoke of before. Which means I'm here because Gregory already had a prior engagement with his regular coven that he needed to make an appearance at to avoid questions. Are the eight members of his secret coven mixed in with the other guests? Will they stay after for the main event? Or does Gregory plan to haul me out to the cabin later? If only I had the potion Donovan and I planned to make. I could sneak it into their cocktails and knock them all out, now.

But the skullcap is back at Barlow Manor, and the potion won't work without it. If only magic worked the way it does in the movies. I'd drop a magical bomb on that pool house, then ride away into the sunset with Donovan. A real bomb would work nicely, too. Maybe we should have focused more on manmade devices instead of a silly potion to knock people out.

Angry to be so close to the enemy and have to leave them alive, I crawl along the edge of the bushes, then dart across the open pathway and behind the house to a familiar patio. Here's where my world fell apart a second time when I witnessed Donovan and Macey being chummy at his dad's party.

What would have happened if I went there on his arm like he originally wanted? Would his father have pretended not to know me? Would he have just made his son's girlfriend quietly disappear and continue on with his plans to groom Donovan to take over his coven? Would Donovan have been swayed while his heart was broken by my abandonment?

This place brings up too many questions I don't want to think about. Our paths didn't go that direction, and it's useless to dwell on what-ifs.

About to dash past the large windows, movement within pulls me up short. I freeze in the shadows as light blooms in the room, illuminating Donovan, and my heart lodges itself in my throat.

No, why is he here? He should be in the mountains searching for me.

I lift a hand to draw his attention, then flinch back into hiding when another figure joins him.

Gregory strides into the room and shuts the door, locking it and stealing my chance to warn Donovan.

8

Gregory says something that pulls Donovan around, and desperate to hear their conversation, I gently prod at the latch on the window, urging it to open so I can push it up a crack to allow their voices to drift out.

"You know you're always welcome, son," Gregory says as he grips Donovan's shoulder. "I've been worried about you over the last year, and when you suddenly vanished at the same time as Macey..."

I will my pulse to slow, for the blood to stop its rush through my veins as I strain to hear past my panic.

"Macey?" Confusion fills Donovan's voice. "What does she have to do with anything? Did you finally let her become a full member of the coven?"

"No, of course not." Gregory studies him for a moment. "She didn't have what we look for in our members."

Donovan chuckles. "You mean she wasn't rich or magically gifted."

His father joins in. "Well, we do need funding, and the rich do like to pretend. Macey was good at drawing in new donors, though, so I was sad when she skipped town."

Donovan shrugs. "I didn't come here to talk about Macey. She wasn't even on my radar past that party. A little too desperate, if you know what I mean."

I shiver to hear Gregory's words coming from Donovan's mouth.

Gregory laughs with appreciation. "I'm glad to know you're not easily swayed by a pretty face."

Donovan strides over to a padded chair near the window and sits. "That's actually what I came here to talk to you about."

Out of his son's view, Gregory checks his watch before he walks over to take the seat opposite Donovan, his back to me. "Oh?"

Donovan sits forward, propping his elbows on his knees and clasping his hands. "You know how I was seeing someone in town, right?"

Gregory nods. "So sorry she couldn't make it to the party."

Slimy liar, I think to myself. *You were* delighted *when I didn't show so you could push Macey on him.*

"Yeah." Donovan drops his head to stare at the floor. "Things got strained with me being away in college and having to hide such an important part of myself. I feel stupid now, but she was part of why I wanted to take time off from school."

"I wondered if she had something to do with it." Gregory reaches across the small space that separates them and pats his shoulder. "You aren't the first man to be led around by a girl."

"Yeah." Donovan nods glumly. "After she didn't bother to come to the party, I started thinking about what I really want from life. I'm sorry I went MIA for a few days, but I wanted to come to a decision on my own."

"That's okay, I'm just glad you're safe and healthy, son. You did have me worried."

"Sorry," Donovan says again, his head lifting. For a heartbeat, his gaze moves past his dad and settles on me. His eyes widen a fraction as he lifts a hand to scrub his face in frustration. "I broke things off with her, because I decided I don't want to live a half-life." He stands and paces with restless energy. "I don't want to lie to the person I'm with about who I am."

Oh, gods, he's doing it. He's going with our plan. But this isn't the right setting, and we're not prepared.

Gregory stands, too. "You know I'll support whatever decision you make, son. I only want your happiness."

Liar. He's only saying that now that Donovan's coming around.

Donovan pauses next to the cracked window and squares his shoulders as he tucks his hands behind his back. "Then, I want in."

My pulse leaps as his fingers uncurl to reveal a small potion bottle. He didn't use the hosting spell like we planned, probably because he didn't know where I was. Reaching my fingers through the crack in the window, I take the bottle from him.

Gregory chuckles. "You know you already have a place by my side in the coven. You'll take it over when it's my time to step down."

"No, I want you to continue my education," Donovan declares as he strides over to stand in front of his father. "I'm not a child, anymore. I'm ready to embrace everything you have to teach me. My focus is no longer split between my love life and embracing my magic, and I want to prove I'm the heir you really want, no matter what it takes."

"That's a bold demand," Gregory says slowly, as if sorting through Donovan's words for a hidden meaning. "Right now, we have a gathering waiting for the evening toast. We can discuss this more after they leave."

Pulse racing, I hurry away from the window and back toward the pool. It won't take long for them to return to the gathering. Skirting along the house, using the bushes for cover, I find the staging area that the caterers set up to bring in the food. Two bottles of red wine sit on a serving tray, ready to be poured, and I quickly divide the contents of the potion bottle between them.

The spell said only a drop was needed to take effect, so a single sip of wine should be enough.

About to slip away once more to find a hiding spot, my eye lands on a rack of uniforms that must have come in from the cleaners. A few spares still hang on the rack, and I grab one close to my size before I duck around the corner of the house and quickly change into it.

The button-up shirt and red vest are a little baggy around my waist. I have to use my belt to keep the black slacks up, but I'll pass at a glance. Thankfully, the uniform also comes with a hat that I can tuck my distinctive hair into. Otherwise, the ash-blond and purple strands would give me away in an instant. I pull my cuffs down to make sure they hide the flash of gold around my wrist. I'm surprised Gregory left it, but maybe he was in too much of a hurry to fully search me. I'm just grateful I still have a link to the gold in the mountain. It makes this feel like slightly less than a suicide run.

Head down, I stride with confidence into the kitchen and grab the serving platter that a frenzied-looking woman shoves at me as she yells, "Where are we at on dinner? We're to serve at eight o'clock sharp!"

"Potatoes coming out now!" a man responds from the ovens as he pulls foil-wrapped potatoes from the oven and tosses them into a bowl.

"Salads ready to be dressed," calls a woman with a large, metal bowl in her hand.

"Salmon will go in as soon as the salads go out!" another yells.

"What are you standing around for, girl?" A shove between my shoulder blades sends me stumbling forward a step, and I almost drop the tray of hors d'oeuvres I hold. "Empty the tray and come right back. As soon as Mr. Crawford returns, we need to have the salad plates going out."

Nodding, I hold the tray in front of my face as I stride out of the side door and across the short distance to the pool house, where another server stands at the door to let me through.

My heart pounds as I step into the room. Even knowing better, I expect for fingers to point and screams that another witch stepped within their midst. Instead, no one even looks at me. I'm a floating try from which they claim their treats as I drift around the room. The uniform I put on might as well have made me invisible.

I pass another server in the room who gives me a curious glance before continuing on her rounds. Does she think I'm a substitute for who the uniform should have belonged to? Was the craziness in the kitchen because they're short-staffed? Luck favored me in this as I make two circuits of the room, peeking at faces to see if I recognize anyone from the group who trekked out to the cabin.

But it was dark, and we were too far away to make out features. As far as I'm concerned though, anyone here with power needs to be neutralized. Even if they don't all know the depths to which Gregory stoops, they must share some of the same beliefs to be part of his coven. And those who just want to pretend to be witches... Magic doesn't belong in the hands of those who don't know how to wield it.

I keep my eyes and ears open for any hint that they plan a dark ritual tonight, but aside from the black table cloth on the center table and the real candles flickering to illuminate the space, it looks like any other social gathering. They must keep the dark service for after all the humans are gone.

When the last hors d'oeuvre vanishes from my tray, I head for the door just as Donovan walks into the room. Our eyes meet, and he quickly turns to the side, allowing his father to walk ahead of me while hiding me from view.

"It's in the wine," I whisper, my voice pitched for his ears alone.

He doesn't acknowledge my words as he turns, and I shuffle behind him, using his broad back to hide my small frame until I can escape out the door and back across the short path. I already took enough of a risk

About to duck around the side of the house, the woman from earlier catches sight of me and gestures me over.

"What are you doing?" she hisses. "Salads have to go out! What company sent you over?"

I mumble under my breath and bob my head as I scurry into the kitchen and load my empty tray with bowls of salad before getting into line behind the other servers and following them back into the pool house.

Everyone now sits around the tables, glasses clinking and quiet conversation still filling the space. Gregory sits at the head of the table, with Donovan in the chair to his right. It's a position of power and earns him more than one frown from the guests. Who did they hope would become Gregory's right hand, knowing he had an heir? And how soon would Donovan have had an *accident* if he truly planned to stay?

Those looks confirm my first instinct that they all need to be stripped of their powers. Combining magic with greed never results in anything good. One of the rules my mother drilled into me that I believe is the rule of three. Whatever you put out there will return three-fold.

Gregory and these people destroyed the covens of mine and Donovan's mother, and we are here to deliver back what they did to us. We won't take their lives from them, though. Only their power. Let them live with the knowledge of what they could have been and hate who they became.

Weak. Powerless. Humans.

I keep my head down as I set bowls of salad in front of each person, working my way down the row of seats on the left. The server ahead of me has started farther down the table, and I breathe easier knowing I won't have to go near Gregory. I don't know what I would do if I stood at his back, but the butter knives on the table hold a tempting allure.

When my tray empties, I force myself to return to the kitchen, where I'm put to work burning my fingers by peeling the foil wrappers from the potatoes and splitting them open, then adding them to the staged plates. Another server walks behind me, adding bowls of butter beside them. The next person adds asparagus, on which the chef gently settles pink strips of salmon.

"Don't spill!" the staff director snaps, and I glance over my shoulder to see another girl filling the wine glasses.

Her hands shake, either from exhaustion or nerves, and a splash of red wine beads on the cart. "I'm sorry, ma'am!"

"Pay attention!" a sharp nudge brings my attention back around, and I hurry to finish the potatoes as I mentally will the girl not to spill any more precious wine.

We don't have a backup if her nerves ruin our plan.

By the time I finish, the cart with the wine has already gone out to the tables, and I gather my assigned plates onto my tray.

As we enter the pool house, Gregory stands at the head of the table, giving a speech about unity and his wish for success for the remainder of the year. It makes me want to gag, as everyone around the table lifts their full wine glasses in salute before taking sips of the red liquid. Like he knows anything about unity. He'd kill every one of them if it meant more power for himself.

Lifting a full plate from my tray, I lean in to set it in front of a white-haired man that looks a lot like the town mayor. As I do, the server next to me fumbles her dish, and the potato rolls off the plate.

The man beside me flinches back, his elbow knocking my hand and sending the contents of the plate across the table.

He turns on me, his face red with embarrassment. "Why, I never. What's your name, girl? I'll have your job for this travesty."

The server who started it backs away, her eyes wide as the attention in the room shifts toward us.

At the end of the table, Donovan pushes back his

chair and stands, lifting his wine glass once more. "I'd like to give another toast, this one to my father."

A few people lift glasses, then hesitate when Gregory ignores his son, his cold gaze narrowed on me. "Take off your hat, child."

Dread pools in my gut as I meet his eyes.

He gives me a cruel smile. "Well, it looks like our guest of honor just couldn't wait for her introduction. Maybe I present Sabine Barlow to the room?"

Slowly, I reach up and tug my hat off, spilling my hair down my back. "I do hope you enjoyed your wine, Gregory."

Realization dawns, and he drops the glass in his hand. "Scott, grab her!"

Dropping the rest of the plates onto the mayor's lap, I slam the side of the tray into his face before he can grab me. Around the room, screams fill the air as people slump face-first into their salmon dinners.

People try to run for the door, but the potion takes them out like dominoes, their bodies falling in untidy rows. Only the servers escape, leaving me, Donovan, and Gregory alone in the chaos.

9

The air rips from my lungs. At first, I think Gregory has done something to me, but then I recognize the feeling as fear. Why didn't he fall with the rest of them?

Dropping the tray, I keep my focus on Gregory to keep my eyes away from Donovan. He must have found my stash if he made the anti-potion, but since his father didn't go down, it would have been better if Donovan did. If he had, he wouldn't be implicated in any of this, safe from his father's retribution.

"What's going on?" Donovan asks as Gregory and I glare at each other.

"You tell me." Gregory glances between us before he grips Donovan's bicep hard enough to make him wince. "Why didn't you pass out with everyone else?"

Worried Gregory will hurt him, I lift my chin. "I didn't want him to pass out. I wanted him to be lucid as I cut his heart out, just like you did with my family. I wanted you to wake to the same devastation I lived through, finding my family butchered by your hand."

Gregory relaxes his grip on his son but doesn't let go. "Is that so? How does it feel to fail? Because I'm still alive, and so is Donovan."

"I may have failed at drugging you, but this isn't over, yet." I lock my legs, fighting the urge to run.

I won't leave Donovan here. What's left of my heart would shatter into a million pieces.

"Stupid girl. Don't you know you've already lost?" Gregory laughs, the sound light instead of the evil cackle I expected. "Did you know, after we extracted your families' hearts and burned them, we placed their bodies in airtight, plastic drums, then dumped them in a mass grave? If you came here hoping to lay them to rest, you've wasted your time."

His words don't bring the pain he hoped for, because I know they're lies. We found the hearts at his cabin, but he doesn't realize we broke into his underground lair. Even if he did dump their bodies in a mass grave, I can still perform the rituals on their hearts.

All is not lost, but he can't know that. My nails dig

into my hands, the pain forcing tears to well in my eyes, and I fake a sob.

He gives me a triumphant smile. "We knew the names of everyone in your coven. We counted the bodies to make sure we captured and killed everyone."

Blood drips from my fists. I should have killed Macey.

"I knew you were missing, but my spells couldn't find you." He swings his arm out wide. "But here you are. You walked right into my house, Sabine Barlow. Were you that desperate to join the rest of your coven?"

Hattie saved us with her foresight when she suggested I use my middle name. She saved me for this moment, so I have to stay focused even though our plot didn't go as planned.

"I plan to live a long, healthy life, knowing you're dead," I counter, trying not to let him know how much he affects me. How his hand around Donovan's arm sends spikes of fear into my heart.

Gregory sneers at me before he looks at Donovan. "You said you wanted me to educate you. Are you prepared to prove your loyalty tonight and join my *real* coven?"

Donovan's eyes jump to me. "What do I have to do?"

"This girl is our enemy." Gregory pulls Donovan along behind him as he strides around the table and toward me. "I guess I shouldn't call you the enemy. You're just a means to an end, albeit a very powerful end."

Donovan's eyes cut to mine briefly. "She must be a powerful witch. She took out the rest of the coven easily."

"Pure luck on her part. You have two options." Gregory's eyes harden on his son. "You can kill her now, we take her heart and drain its power, and you join the coven, or we keep her around, so she can produce strong Crawford heirs, then we dispose of her."

"Neither I nor my children will ever bow to you," I spit.

Having children means I'm still alive, but I'd die before leaving them to a life managed by this man.

"This isn't your call. You're lucky I'd even consider the option, not that you would have much of a life other than as an incubator." Gregory shifts his focus back to Donovan. "Choose."

"I..." Donovan draws out.

He won't look at me, and I can only imagine

what's going through his head. Offering to keep me alive to be a *human incubator* gives us a chance to fight another day, but we both know that Gregory won't let that happen. Once we're in his clutches, we'll be nothing more than a shell of what we were.

"Well?" Gregory's voice hardens.

Donovan's eyes meet mine, his expression inscrutable. "I'll kill her now."

Even knowing he's playing along with his father, hearing him say those words makes my stomach tighten in dread. We're ending this here. One way or another. No turning back.

"That's a shame, but I respect your choice." Gregory squeezes Donovan's arm. "Keeping her around would have just given her hope, anyway. Now, you show her what happens to people who mess with the Crawfords."

Gregory releases him, and Donovan strides to the table to grab a steak knife from beside one of the fallen coven members. I'm not sure how long they'll be out, and their bodies will get in the way of a fight.

As Donovan faces me, the knife in his hand, a niggle of doubt creeps in that this has all been a trick.

"Oh, don't be barbaric." Gregory turns away,

reaching from something that was beside his plate. "Use this, instead."

As Gregory turns back to us, his hand out, Donovan strikes, hitting his father in the side, the blade sliding into his flesh. My mind blanks momentarily, then guilt crushes in on me for doubting Donovan. He was just buying us time, getting his father to let his guard down.

I don't have time to dwell on that, though, as Gregory yanks the sheath off the ceremonial blade in his hand—no, *my family's athame*—and slashes at Donovan.

Donovan dodges to the side, the steak knife shaking in his hand as he faces his father.

"You're working with her?" Gregory spits out, his features twisted. "I should have known you were too weak. Just like your mother."

"I know what you did to my mother and to Evaine's family." Donovan swipes at his father, the two men circling. "I could never join you."

"Evaine, huh?" Gregory's lip curls. "So that's how she evaded me all these years. Is this the girlfriend you told me about? Pathetic. You'll die right alongside her."

Rage builds within me, and the air fills with static. But my legs refuse to move, my feet stuck to the floor. Looking down, I notice small runes as the pattern in the carpet.

How stupid of me to think this man wouldn't be prepared for anything.

I pound my hands together in frustration, and the cuff of my borrowed shirt slides up to reveal my gold cuff, reminding me my magic is enhanced. If I focus, I can beat Gregory. The wounds left by my nails on my palms are still raw, and I pick at them until they bleed again. The blood drips through my fingers to pool on the carpet as I move my hand to draw the rune to block magic. Unsure if it will work, I draw on the gold, power racing through my veins. As I finish, the rune glows, blocking the spell in the carpet so I can move once more.

With Gregory focused on Donovan, I try to sneak around behind him, but Gregory's prepared, shooting a fireball at my face. I send blessings to Hattie for teaching me to fight this magic as I capture the fireball and send it back his way.

The fire sails through the air, and Donovan uses the distraction to stab his father again, this time in the leg. As Gregory spins to face Donovan, the fireball hits an invisible shield, and sparks fly, igniting the carpet and tablecloth. With so much flammable material in here, the fire quickly grows, and soon, smoke fills the room.

The passed-out witches don't even twitch as the fire begins to consume those closest to it, the scent of burned meat filling the air. My stomach clenches at the stench, and I drop to my knees as my stomach heaves. We never planned to kill anyone, and Gregory does nothing to stop it as he pins Donovan to the ground, the two men struggling with the athame.

Reaching out to the raging fire, I pull it into myself and throw it at Gregory's back.

Unprepared for the attack, the fire hits him, and his jacket ignites. Flinching upright, Gregory struggles out of his jacket, and Donovan wrestles the athame from his hand and slips out from beneath his father.

Donovan runs to the opposite side of the room from where I stand and holds up the hand with his mother's ring on it. Somehow in their struggle, Donovan created containment runes, and he now activates them with his blood. Backed by his mother's magic, the spell should be strong enough to hold Gregory, at least temporarily.

"Sabine," Donovan calls, "stay there and be ready. We have to say the binding spell quickly."

Donovan doesn't wait for me to answer as he drops his mom's ring on the table and races over to complete the triangle.

I send prayers up to all the goddesses, asking them to bless us, but will they answer as we perform these spells not just out of desperation but also hate and vengeance? We may be on our own, but it won't stop us from trying.

"Feed your magic through the ring. I'll do the same and use it as a conduit to link us." I cast out my magic, the gold on my wrist seeking out the gold we bound to the ring. It would be better if we were touching, but with so many people to capture in our web, the space is necessary.

Gregory screams at us, but we ignore him, our eyes locked on each other and our magic humming through the triangle we created.

As I start the spell, the magic in the people around us glows. Many have dark or nearly black auras around them. My magic shies away from their taint, but I hold firm, pulling from my family magic that's been locked inside of me. Those closest to the door have the lightest of magic, and those wink out first. Many of his strongest followers were toward the front, but since they're passed out, they aren't able to fight the spell.

With only Gregory left, we close in around him, our magic swelling as we move closer together.

"You won't succeed! This binding may work now, but I'm stronger than you. Once I'm free, I'll remove the spell and hunt you down until your heart is on display in my office," Gregory spits at Donovan.

"I know," Donovan says as he lunges forward and drives the knife he holds straight into his father's heart. "That's why I can't let you live."

Gregory grasps at Donovan's hand, but blood bubbles from his lips. Donovan pulls the knife out and pushes his father into the flames that are building with intensity. Gregory's green eyes widen as he crashes into the flames, his arms spread out from his sides as if to embrace death or maybe the pain that goes along with it.

"I had to do it," Donovan murmurs, his expression bleak as he trembles. "I couldn't let him keep hurting people. He would never have stopped."

Not knowing how to respond, I link my fingers through his and squeeze. He doesn't return the gesture, but the shaking slows. "I'm sorry you're the one who did it. I was ready to deal the blow."

Donovan's glassy eyes scan the room. "You need to run. The fire department will have already been alerted to the fire. They'll be here soon, and you can't get caught." He pushes me toward the door.

"What about you?" I chew my lip, not wanting to leave him.

"I'm going to go sit back at my spot at the table and pretend to be passed out. The smoke will probably help me pass out to make it look real." He directs me to the door again.

I grab his hand to pull him with me. "I don't like that plan. You may not make it back out of here."

He kisses my temple and gives me a sad smile. "People saw me here."

"People saw me, too," I protest.

"But no one knows who you are. Lay low at the campsite, and I'll come find you when it's safe." He pushes me again. "Now, please go."

The sound of sirens reaches my ears, and I know I have to make a quick decision. "I'll put the sleeping spell on you, otherwise, they'll know you're faking it. Go sit in your chair."

Donovan frowns but does as I ask. Once he's seated, I perform the spell, and he slumps over the table. The sirens grow louder, and the fire is far enough away from him that he should be safe until help arrives. Heart pounding, I run to the side door and slip out of the building and into the trees at the back of the property. There, I climb one of the trees to get a better view of the pool house.

The firetrucks pull in from the service driveway, and firemen pile out and are in action within minutes of parking.

I wait and watch, thinking the entire time about Donovan and what comes next for us.

EPILOGUE

"Back it up!" Donovan yells as he beckons for me to keep backing up the truck.

Since the trailer blocks most of my vision, I inch backward at a snail's pace, terrified I'll knock something over.

When Donovan suggested we haul the old thing down from the mountains, I resisted at first, worried we may need it sometime in the future. But he convinced me that leaving it abandoned would draw more attention to the hidden gold than moving it down to Barlow Manor. Besides, we may have to sleep in it for a while as we fix up the house.

An entire season passed since the fire that killed Donovan's father and a number of his guests. The fire department ultimately ruled it a terrible accident, and the servers who came forward mysteriously lost their memories of the night. In fact, most of the guests had amnesia, which the doctors attributed to trauma from the fire. They may have had some help of magic to come to that decision, and slowly, Manberry moved on from the story of the fire at the Crawford house.

Donovan inherited his father's land business and sold off a large portion of it, but not the part that held a claim on Barlow Manor and its properties. We spun the story of my disappearance all those years ago as traveling around the world. My family's reclusive nature meant nobody really asked questions about my return, and those who it really mattered to knew what really happened.

A few Moon witches reached out, offering to take over where my mother left off, but I politely declined. I had no plans to continue in my family's footsteps. Hattie showed me there was a gap in how witches identified their magic, and I planned to fill that gap with Donovan's help.

"Stop!" Donovan shouts.

I put the truck into park and open the door. Maggie bolts across my lap and vanishes into the overgrown grass as I hop out.

I study the placement. "Are you sure this is where we should put it?"

We decided to park the trailer near the old garage, out of the way of the house. It offered privacy and wouldn't be seen from the street, but it also made it feel like we're crouching on the outskirts instead of reclaiming the land.

Donovan wraps his arms around me from behind. "Do you want the apprentices to come knocking whenever they want?"

"We don't even have apprentices," I scoff as I lean back against his firm chest. "For all we know, we'll be the only ones living here."

"We'll have apprentices." He props his chin on my shoulder. "The website is getting a lot of traction."

While we waited for the dust to settle, Donovan and I worked on digitizing the grimoires from both of our families, finding many similarities between our books. Not the dark grimoire, though. It vanished from the trailer after the fire at Donovan's house and stayed gone even when I tried to summon it. Maybe that means I'm no longer the right witch for it, and it's done stalking me.

Vengeance no longer fills my heart, and I've found happiness with who I am. Taking down

Gregory didn't magically take away the grief over losing my family, but it brought peace to know he would never do to another coven what he did to mine.

I turn my head, my nose bumping against Donovan's face. "Do you think anything would grow if we planted it now?"

"We should wait until construction's done on the house. Hopefully, we'll be in before winter." He shivers against me. "I don't want to be sleeping out here with no heat."

"It's not that bad." I hug his arms around me. "Lots of snuggling."

"My feet hang off the end of the bed," he grumbles.

"I'll keep them warm." I step on his hard boot to show how good I'll be at warming his feet.

He laughs before he releases me. "We should get ready."

My throat tightens, and I nod.

Together, we walk to his SUV and pull out the large trunk in the back, then carefully make our way through the overgrown fields to the house.

We set the trunk down on the back patio, where we set up an altar and pyre earlier. Moving the trailer hadn't been our only adventure today. We had also made a stop at his father's cabin early this morning and emptied out the underground lair. Much of it we destroyed, but some were too precious, even with the darkness it held. Those items were now locked up safely in the vault in the library. But this trunk we kept with us.

Now, as the sun heads toward the treeline, we light the pyre and make our offerings at the altar, chanting to the Horned God to welcome our families to the Summerland, along with all those who Gregory killed for their power.

Before we packed the hearts into the trunks, we added herbs and sacred crystals to honor the dead. Now, we each take a side and move the heavy trunk onto the small platform we built. The flames beneath it rise as if to embrace them, and we step back.

Our fingers twine together as we stand in silence, watching the trunk burn and finally freeing the souls of those who were trapped for so long.

A gust of sweet-smelling wind rushes past us, fanning the flames higher. I imagine I hear children laughing and the patter of small feet on the stones running past, and I smile.

Donovan nudges his arm against mine. "What are you thinking?"

"I hope we have a lot of apprentices." My eyes

burn as I stare into the fire. "This house needs more than just us."

"They'll come, and we'll be here to welcome them," he says with such assurance that I expect them to appear on the spot.

Instead, a meow draws my eyes to the woods, and I spot a white tail moving through the tall grass.

A moment later, Maggie trots into the garden, a trio of gray kittens scampering behind her.

My free hand lifts to my mouth as tears sting my eyes.

"It's a sign of a new beginning," Donovan whispers as he crouches, holding out his hand and one of the kittens bumps her small head against his fingers. He looks up at me, love shining in his eyes. "For both of us."

"Yeah." The wood of the pyre cracks, sending sparks into the darkening sky.

Barlow Manor won't be the same place I grew up in, but Donovan and I will build a new home here for all the witches who feel like they don't belong, just as we did. And we'll make sure it's filled with love, laughter, and hope.

From death came a new beginning that I plan to seize with both hands and never let go.

ABOUT THE AUTHOR

Lili Black is the young adult, paranormal romance pen name of authors LA Kirk and Lyn Forester.

For More About These Authors, Check Out
www.authorliliblack.com

Made in the USA
Middletown, DE
14 February 2022